North Woods Girl

With all my love to Bryan, and to Maureen and Aliza, my own north woods girls. —AB

In memory of Elsie Hazen, a north woods girl in spirit all her 108 years. —CM

www.mnhspress.org

The Minnesota Historical Society Press is a member of the Association of American University Presses.

Book design by Christa Schneider, Mighty Media
The illustrations in this book were rendered in scratchboard, dyes and watercolors.

Manufactured in Canada

10 9 8 7 6 5 4 3 2 1

♾ The paper used in this publication meets the minimum requirements of the American National Standard for Information Sciences—Permanence for Printed Library Materials, ANSI Z39.48-1984.

International Standard Book Number
ISBN: 978-0-87351-966-3 (cloth)

Library of Congress Cataloging-in-Publication Data
Bissonette, Aimée M.
    North woods girl / Aimée Bissonette ; illustrations by Claudia McGehee.
      pages cm
    Summary: "An admiring granddaughter hikes in all seasons with Grandma, the quintessential north woods girl. Together they see squirrels gathering nuts, hear wood frogs peep, inhale piney scents, and choose the finest skipping stone"—Provided by publisher.
    ISBN 978-0-87351-966-3 (cloth : alk. paper)
    [1. Forests and forestry—Fiction. 2. Nature—Fiction. 3. Seasons—Fiction. 4. Grandmothers—Fiction. 5. Minnesota—Fiction.] I. McGehee, Claudia, 1963–, illustrator. II. Title.
    PZ7.1.B56No 2015
    [E]—dc23
                                               2015001273

North Woods Girl

AIMÉE BISSONETTE *with illustrations by* CLAUDIA McGEHEE

MINNESOTA
HISTORICAL
SOCIETY PRESS

My grandma says she's not a good-looking woman.

I don't know. She looks pretty good to me.

She is not like other grandmas, it's true.

She's bony.

And she dresses in Grandpa's old flannel shirts.

And she never bakes cookies or gooey berry pies.

But when Grandma tucks her pants into her oversized boots and grabs her walking stick, I run to catch up.

There are a hundred little paths in the woods behind
Grandma's house, and Grandma knows them all.

In the spring, Grandma and I trudge through the mud to the pond, binoculars around our necks. We look for the ducks that migrate through on their way further north: buffleheads and teals, goldeneyes and mergansers.

We listen to the wood frogs *peep, peep, peep* as we sit on "Grandpa's log." A long time ago when Grandpa was still alive, he dragged it from the woods for us.

In the summer, Grandma and I work in her garden.
We grow fat red tomatoes and green string beans to can
and give as gifts to Grandma's neighbors and friends.

When the day heats up, we head for
the cool shade of the woods. Grandma says
I must be a north woods girl, just like her. Neither of
us can stand the heat. She's right. But mostly, I like to
breathe in the woods' pine scent. The smell tickles
my nose. It smells like Grandma.

On our walks in the fall, we see signs of the coming winter. Squirrels gather acorns and seeds. Large flocks of Canada geese fly over our heads.

Honk, honk, honk.

The fat cattails by the pond swell and pop, and their fuzzy seeds scatter with the wind. Grandma and I skip stones across the pond.

One, two, three, four, five.

Grandma smiles, her blue eyes crinkling
at the corners. Winter is coming.
And Grandma and I think
winter is best of all.

On winter nights, when the moon is full
and I am lucky enough to be at Grandma's,
Grandma and I bundle up and make our way through the
snowy woods. The bright moon above the trees throws inky shadows across our
path. We talk in whispers, our boots crunching and squeaking in the cold snow.
Sometimes we scare up rabbits and deer, sometimes a red fox.

At the pond, I dust the snow off Grandpa's log. We sit and listen for hooting owls until we ache from the cold, our breath rising up to the stars. Then back to Grandma's we go, where Mom has a pot of chili simmering on the stove.

Mom wants Grandma to move to the city with us.
She worries about Grandma living alone in the woods.

But what would happen if we took that north woods girl away from her woods?

Grandma is staying put. She has a neighbor who plows her driveway and shovels a path to her door. She makes her own path back to the woods. She keeps it clear with daily walking for the next time I come to stay.

My grandma says she is not a good-looking woman.

I don't know. She looks pretty good to me.

She is not like other grandmas, it's true.

Some day, I hope to be just like her.